NOT SO Different

Written by Cyana Riley
Illustrated by Anastasia Kanavaliuk

 notsodifferentbook   anaoseynn

THIS BOOK BELONGS TO

_____

_____

First published in 2020
Printed in the United States

Written by : Cyana Riley
(IG/FB: @notsodifferentbook)

Cover page/Illustrations: Anastasia Kanavaliuk
(IG: @anaoseynn)

ISBN: 978-0-578-69099-5 (paperback)

Published by GreyNash, LLC.

www.notsodifferentbook.com

To Hunter and Teagan, my reasons for everything. Always remember, the things that make you different, also make you special. To the love of my life, Doug, thank you for always believing in me and never letting me give up on my dreams.

HUNTER

TEAGAN

My hair is kinky curly,
your hair is silky straight.
Even though they're different,
they both are really great!

The world needs different people, it's called diversity.
Let's shout out loud about it, it's up to you and me!

Let's celebrate our differences
and spread our love around.
Deep inside of each of us,
so much love can be found.

And since we are all different,
it is the way to be.
I can learn from you,
and you can learn from me!

It doesn't seem like fun
to have only friends like you,
so go find someone different
and make them your friend too!

And even though we're different,
some things are still alike.
We can both love red,
we both love riding on our bike.

So yes, everyone is different,
we are all different this is true.
But just because we're different,
does not mean I can't love you,

Breakout children's book author, Cyana Riley was born and raised in Washington, D.C.. She graduated from George Washington University and spent the first 6 years of her career as a preschool teacher. It was during that time when she fell in love with writing and sharing children stories.

Made in the USA
Middletown, DE
25 May 2021